A CHRISTMAS PROMISE

LARK CARRIER

PICTURE BOOK STUDIO

Amy has been waiting a whole year for the day when Father will bring her Tree indoors to be decorated with the shiny balls and twinkling lights of Christmas.

All year long she has been watching over the Tree, making sure it would be ready.

Now she hears her father's voice.

Amy!

Wake up!
It's the day to bring in
your Christmas Tree.

Oh! Great!

I hope everyone has
moved out of my Tree.
They all promised, but
I'd better go and look.

Hello! Hello!
Anyone here?
Hello! Hello!

But no one answers.

It's so quiet!

Suddenly feeling sad and
all alone, Amy thinks of
all her friends who have
lived in her Tree.

Where are they now?
she wonders.

Laughing out loud she
remembers how Mr. and
Mrs. Blue Jay squabbled
with the Red Cards over
who could live in the
green treetop.

What a noise!

*Luckily my Tree had two
good views at the top.
So I told the Blue Jays
and the Red Cards they
could both stay, but they
had to promise to move
by Christmas.*

They promised.

So when the Yellow
Finches arrived there
was only a small uproar
until they settled into the
lower branches.

I also told them they
had to promise to move
by Christmas.

They promised, too.
Soon my Tree was
swaying as if it was
dizzy from all the
bright flashing wings,
the coming and going,
as the Blue Jays and the
Red Cards and the
Yellow Finches fed their
little ones.

What a commotion!

One day a Golden Turkey
made a shaky landing,
creating quite a stir.

He said he'd be coming
often to rest in my Tree
after his feasts in the
corn field.

I decided a little tree-
shaking was not so bad
though he did knock some
pine cones off.

So I said it was fine, but
he'd have to promise to
stop before Christmas.

He promised.

Then...
Rat–a–tat–tat!

What a headache!

That was the day Silver
Beak decided to clean
my Tree. He worked all
day and then said the job
wasn't finished. He'd
have to stay longer.

I said that was fine,
but he'd have to hurry up –
and promise to be done
by Christmas.

He promised

When Orange Eyes
arrived everyone made
quite a fuss about his
hoo–ooting lullaby, but
soon they all slept
better, knowing he was
keeping guard.

But I had to make
him promise to move
by Christmas, too.

He promised.

On the day White
Stripes arrived we ran
for our lives…

What a smell!

When we finally came
back he explained that our
noise had scared him and
made him lose control.
But he said it wouldn't
happen again.

So everyone decided
he and his family could
move into the lower trunk
of the Tree, as long as
they promised to move
out by Christmas.

They promised.

The noisiest day ever was when the Gray Chatters arrived. They were yelling loudly about something none of us understood.

But when White Stripes flashed his threatening tail, they quieted down quickly!

Then everyone agreed the Gray Chatters could have the lower roots of the Tree for storing the fallen pine cones they had gathered.

But they had to promise to leave by Christmas.

They promised.

Slippery Green scared
me the first time I saw
him silently twine himself
around the Tree trunk on
his way to catch a bit
of sun.

Since there was plenty
of room in the Tree's
mysterious root caves,
it was decided Slippery
and his wife could stay
there. It was nice having
a quiet family around;
but they had to promise to
move by Christmas.

They promised.

Even at my picnics, I was busy telling everyone to move by Christmas.

There were the Ants, who enjoyed running up and down the trunk carrying specks of bark.

There were the Butterflies, who rode the Tree's swaying limbs.

And there were all the bright, shiny Beetles, who slowly roamed the dark roots, taking flight from time to time.

They all promised.

But now, what silence!

*All my friends have
really moved! They have
all kept their promises.*

What have I done?

But there is no answer.
Now Amy grows even
lonelier and sadder.
She is quiet for a long
time, thinking.
Then Amy makes a Very
Loud Speech.

PLEASE LISTEN!

*If you all come back I will
not take the Tree indoors.*

*It's your Tree, forever,
not mine.*

I promise!

Amy waits, but still there
is no answer.

That night is Christmas
Eve. Amy goes to bed but
she can't sleep.

This is horrible, she thinks,
No noise…
no friends…
no Christmas Tree…
no…
…What's that?

TAP... TAP!

Amy runs to the window.

There is her Tree.
But she has never seen it
looking so beautiful.

Oh, you're back,
you're all back!
And you'll never have to
leave again, I promise!

Merry Christmas, Amy!

Merry Christmas, everyone!

*The original art for A CHRISTMAS PROMISE was done in pastels
and colored pencils on handmade paper made from bleached blue jeans
by Rugg Road Handmade Paper, Allston, Massachusetts.*

Copyright © 1986 Lark Carrier
Published by PICTURE BOOK STUDIO,
an imprint of Neugebauer Press, Salzburg–Munich–London–Boston.
Distributed in USA by Alphabet Press, Natick, MA.
Distributed in Canada by Vanwell Publishing, St. Catharines.
Distributed in UK by Ragged Bears, Andover.
All rights reserved.
Printed in Austria.

LIBRARY OF CONGRESS CATALOGING IN PUBLICATION DATA

Carrier, Lark, 1947–
A Christmas promise.

*Summary: Amy makes all the animal inhabitants promise
to leave a tree by Christmas so she can bring it indoors
to decorate, but on the day they depart, she is overcome by
the silence and her loneliness.*
[1. Animals—Fiction. 2. Trees—Fiction.
Christmas—Fiction] I. Title.
PZ7.C23453Ch 1986 [E] 86-12356
ISBN 0-88708-032-4

*Ask your bookseller for this other PICTURE BOOK STUDIO book
by Lark Carrier: THERE WAS A HILL....*